For Sam,
who is truly
unique! A.B.

For Erin
and Isla
S.R.

OXFORD
UNIVERSITY PRESS

Great Clarendon Street, Oxford OX2 6DP

Oxford University Press is a department of the University of Oxford.
It furthers the University's objective of excellence in research, scholarship,
and education by publishing worldwide in

Oxford   New York

Auckland   Cape Town   Dar es Salaam   Hong Kong   Karachi
Kuala Lumpur   Madrid   Melbourne   Mexico City   Nairobi
New Delhi   Shanghai   Taipei   Toronto

With offices in

Argentina   Austria   Brazil   Chile   Czech Republic   France   Greece
Guatemala   Hungary   Italy   Japan   Poland   Portugal   Singapore
South Korea   Switzerland   Thailand   Turkey   Ukraine   Vietnam

Oxford is a registered trade mark of Oxford University Press
in the UK and in certain other countries

Text © Ann Bonwill 2013
Illustrations © Simon Rickerty 2013
Photograph on page 4 © Stephane Angue /Shutterstock.com

The moral rights of the author/illustrator have been asserted

Database right Oxford University Press (maker)

First published in 2013

British Library Cataloguing in Publication Data available

ISBN: 978-0-19-274544-6 (hardback)
ISBN: 978-0-19-274545-3 (paperback)

2 4 6 8 10 9 7 5 3 1

Printed in China

Paper used in the production of this book is a natural,
recyclable product made from wood grown in sustainable forests.
The manufacturing process conforms to the environmental
regulations of the country of origin

I am not a copycat!

featuring **Hugo** and **Bella**

Ann Bonwill &
Simon Rickerty

OXFORD
UNIVERSITY PRESS

I am Hugo the hippo.
I'm one of a kind.
I am unique!

Thank you! But as I was saying, before I was so rudely interrupted . . .

I'm practising moves for my water ballet.

I don't know another hippo who can . . .

Touch his toes . . .

Nope, can't think of anyone.
Great goggles!

Or even do the splits!

It's true. There's no one like you: you are unique. Right down to your flippers.

I would be, except that **YOU** keep copying me!

WOW! Nice armbands.
Where are we going?

Not telling. And you
are **not** going.

Time for my show.
See how I can float?

So can I!

And dive?

Me, too!

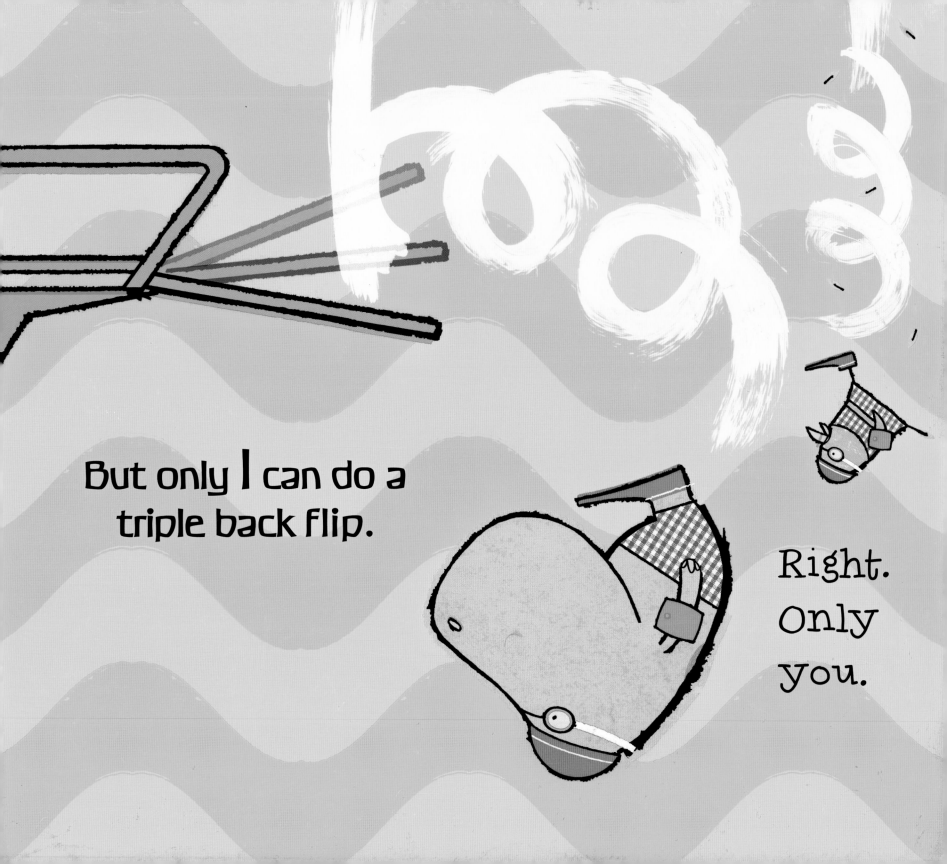

But only I can do a
triple back flip.

Right.
Only
you.

Bella, will you **stop** being a copycat!

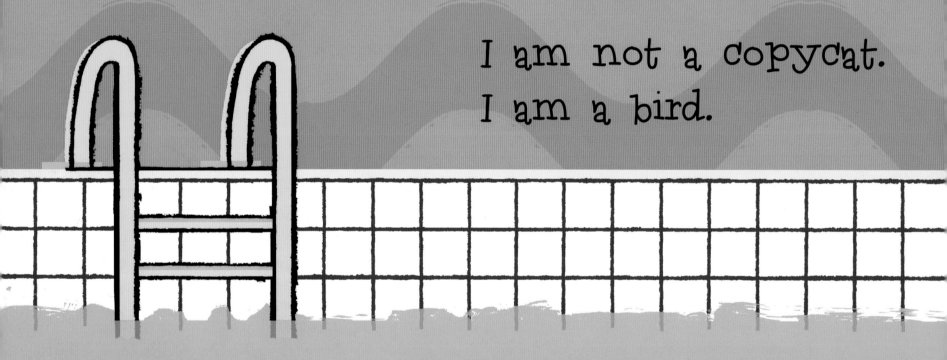

I am not a copycat. I am a bird.

'Bravo!' says another hippo.
'May I take your photo?
You two are amazing
synchronized swimmers!'

'I agree,'
says another
bird. 'Your team is
truly unique!'

See, Hugo, I wasn't ruining your ballet. I was making it better!

I'll have strawberry swirl
with vanilla wafers and
minty sprinkles.

And I'll have
exactly the same!

...double
chocolate chip.

APR - 8 2013